Biscuit's
Big Friend

MY FIRST

I Can Read Book®

Biscuit's Big Friend

story by ALYSSA SATIN CAPUCILLI
pictures by PAT SCHORIES

SCHOLASTIC INC.

New York Toronto London Auckland Sydney
Mexico City New Delhi Hong Kong Buenos Aires

ISBN 0-439-76239-1

Text copyright © 2003 by Alyssa Satin Capucilli. Illustrations copyright © 2003 by Pat Schories. All rights reserved. Published by Scholastic Inc., 557 Broadway, New York, NY 10012, by arrangement with HarperCollins Publishers. SCHOLASTIC and associated logos are trademarks and/or registered trademarks of Scholastic Inc.

36 35 34 33   16/0

Printed in the U.S.A.   40

First Scholastic printing, February 2005

I Can Read Book® is a trademark of HarperCollins Publishers Inc.

This is Biscuit
and his friend Sam.

Biscuit is a small puppy.

Woof, woof!

Sam is a big dog.

Ruff!

Biscuit and Sam
are good friends.

Ruff!

Sam can run fast.

Woof, woof!

Biscuit wants to run fast, too!

Ruff!

Sam can carry a big stick.

Woof, woof!
Biscuit wants to carry
a big stick, too.

Woof, woof!
Ruff!

Biscuit and Sam
want to play tug.

Here, Biscuit!

Here, Sam!

It is time for a drink.

Splash!
Silly puppy!
Sam's dish is too big
for you!

Woof, woof!

Ruff!

Biscuit and Sam
want to play fetch.

Ready?

Fetch!

Uh-oh! There goes the ball!
Now what will we do?

Wait, Sam!

That fence is too big for you!

Woof!

Oh, Biscuit!

Sam is a big friend,
but only a small puppy
like you could do that!

Ruff!

Woof, woof!